LITTLE FARMER
OF THE
MIDDLE WEST

NEBRASKA STATE CAPITOL, LINCOLN, NEBRASKA

LITTLE FARMER OF THE MIDDLE WEST

BY

MADELINE BRANDEIS

Photographic Illustrations

GROSSET & DUNLAP
PUBLISHERS   NEW YORK

CONTENTS

CONTENTS

LITTLE FARMER OF THE MIDDLE WEST
WAS DECORATED BY:

ROBERT BUTTERFIELD, who posed as DAVID

PATRICIA MARTIN, who posed as DOT

ESTELLE ROSENFIELD, who changed herself into AUNT SOPHIE

JOE SHAWN, who was BIG BILL

JOHN BURKARD and JANE BIZZELLE, who were TED AND TESS

JOHN CLARK RENSHAW JR., who was the BABY

To all of you, including Miss Ruth O'Bierne and Mr. M. U. Blumenthal, who made it possible for me to know you, a world of thanks.

MADELINE BRANDEIS

THE LITTLE FARMER OF THE MIDDLE WEST

LITTLE FARMER OF THE MIDDLE WEST

CHAPTER I

THE PLANTING

Little David could hardly wait for dinner to be over. He wanted to go outside again and look at the tiny, new cottonwood trees. He and his father had just planted a long, slender row of them as a windbreak on their farm.

Something inside of David always made music when things were planted. That was why this seemed a glorious day to the sturdy little son of a Nebraska pioneer. He did not know what a really dreadful day it was going to be.

"The Indians have been making trouble

again," said David's father. A large mouthful of buffalo meat disappeared inside of him. "Workers on the Union Pacific Railroad have been killed, and many cabins about here have been burned."

Uncle Will gave him a look of alarm. Uncle Will had arrived only today from the California gold mines. He had brought with him a fortune in gold.

The Harper family sat grouped about a rough table, at their midday meal. The room was used for cooking, living, sleeping —in fact, for everything, because it was the only room in the house. It was now full of steam and loud talk.

Everybody chattered excitedly, for the family had suddenly become rich with the gold that Uncle Will had brought. Tomorrow he would take it to the nearest settlement and put it safely away in a bank.

But tomorrow was still a long way off. And even as they sat planning how to spend their new-found wealth, a band of savage Indians crouched near by. They were watching the log cabin.

As soon as the meal was over, David went outside to the row of young trees. Some day those delicate trunks would be so strong that they would protect the farmhouse from icy winds.

David thought that it would be much the same with a little boy like himself. For, some day his small arms would get brawny and then he would protect his family by working the land and making things grow.

If you had looked deep into David's eyes, you might have seen a long line of prairie wagons crossing the plains. You might have seen the spirit of pioneers.

As David dreamed of the growing of his land, he did not hear another sound far off across the prairies—a sound of hideous yelling.

His family inside the log house did hear it,

however, and everyone jumped up from the table in terror.

"Indians!" they gasped in one breath.

"The gold!" cried Uncle Will. "Quick! Hide it underground!"

Swiftly they started to dig a hole in the hard earth floor of the cabin. Beads of sweat stood out upon their foreheads as they dug. Finally the hole was deep enough.

They lowered the heavy sacks of golden nuggets into the ground and covered them over. Then, grabbing their guns, they prepared to defend their home.

"Where is David?" cried his mother.

All at once she had realized that the boy was not there. He had gone outside and, even now, he would be in the path of those howling redskins!

But David was not aware of his danger. Neither was he aware of his family's distress, nor of how they had hidden the sacks of gold.

He always disliked staying cooped up indoors. He loved the vast, green bigness of the open land, with its wild perfume. He even loved its cruelty.

Sometimes the prairie bellowed thunder and spat flood; it belched dust and screamed cyclone. Yet, to David, it was a splendid savage whom he meant one day to tame.

A shrill cry made him turn around. There, along the river, ran the redskins, their tomahawks raised, their black braids flying. They were making straight for his father's cabin—straight for the only home that David had ever known!

They would break in and would steal Uncle Will's gold. Worse than that, they might even murder his whole family. Oh, if only David could do something to help!

Now they were surrounding the cabin and a shot rang out. Another shot and then another, and one of the Indians fell. But the deafening howls continued as they began to batter in the door with their tomahawks.

David ran toward the little log stable where his father kept a gun. He grabbed it blindly, but when he came out again, not an Indian was in sight. They had entered the cabin and, almost at once, David saw flames and smoke rise up into the sky. His home was burning!

Late that night, a settler, who lived near by, found David beside his row of cotton-wood trees. He stood like a lone soldier, an empty gun in his hand, the tears dried upon his cheeks.

He was looking out across the prairies, beyond the smoking ruins of his father's cabin. He was now the only one left of a brave pioneer family, and he must carry on.

But David did not know that, hidden under the ground where the cabin had stood, lay a fortune in gold!

CHAPTER II

THE CROP

Years have passed and another Harper family now lives on the same farm. But to-day the country looks different. There are no more savage Indians lurking about. Modern houses, windmills, and stables dot the rolling land. In place of shaggy buffalo, graze sleek and peaceful cows.

The Harpers' dirty white farmhouse sprawls beside a dry cornfield. Smoke curls lazily up from its chimney. A weathervane glitters upon the roof of the old red barn.

It is a neglected-looking farm, for these Harpers are very poor. They do not know that under the ground, where the old pioneer cabin once stood, there still lies buried that fortune in gold.

15

One evening at sunset, David Harper the Third came over the hill, bringing in the herd. He was the grandson of that little boy who, so many years ago, had watched his family's cabin being burned to the ground by Indians.

This modern David stood for a moment on the top of the hill. He gazed down at the dry creek bed and at the row of great cottonwood trees, which his grandfather, that other David, had planted.

The cattle lowed, their bells jangling, as David started down the hill and saw his sister running up to meet him. Her brown braids were blowing behind her and little clouds of dust rose up under her flying feet.

"David! David!" she called excitedly. She looked troubled and afraid.

"What's the matter, Dot?" he asked, as he joined her.

"A letter came!" She took his arm, and they started walking toward home together.

Courtesy of J. I. Case Company

A MID-WESTERN FARM

"Oh, and, Davie, Mother cried over it!"

David was a year younger than Dot, but they were close friends.

"I've a notion it's something mighty bad, Davie!" she continued. "When Pa came back from the fields, Ma showed it to him and he frowned. He said, 'We must! We must! There's no help for it!' Oh, Davie, what did he mean by that?"

David had a terrible thought. Lately, his father had been talking about giving up the land and moving to the city. During the twelve years of David's life there had been blizzards, drought, dust storms, and cyclones, and Father Harper had become discouraged.

But David saw promise in the land just as his grandfather had seen it. The spirit of pioneers had settled in David's heart.

He did not answer his sister and suddenly she stopped and pointed to a black cloud frowning in the midst of the glowing sunset.

"Look," she said. "A storm, I expect."

"No," said David, and shook his head. "More likely, just rain, and we sure need it!"

When they reached the farmhouse David and Dot found their mother bent over the stove. The kitchen smelled of fried potatoes and ham.

Father Harper sat in a corner, his head drooping wearily. Even his faded blue shirt looked tired. The small room seemed alive with young Harpers of different ages. There were six of them.

"Supper's ready," said Mother Harper, and they seated themselves noisily about the table.

Father Harper cleared his throat. "I've something important to say to you all," he began, and the noise ceased.

David felt a strange, cold fear. He looked across at Dot.

"Some few weeks ago," went on Father Harper, "I wrote to your aunt Sophie."

Aunt Sophie was Father Harper's sister, who lived in the city of Omaha. She was a very wealthy woman.

"I thought likely she might help us out in our trouble," he continued. "And, well, to-day I got her answer."

All the young eyes asked Father Harper the same question: "What did she say?"

"Aunt Sophie is right willin' to send us

money," he told them. Then he cleared his throat again. "If," he added, "we'll give her one of our children to adopt!"

A horrified gasp went round the table.

"Aunt Sophie's real lonely," broke in Mother Harper, but the tears were showing in her eyes. "And it does seem like a good chance for one of you to go to the city and be educated."

Dot saw David shudder. How dreadful it would be, she thought, if their parents should choose David to go! No, he must never be torn from the soil. Why, he was a part of it. Even his unkempt crop of hair was the color of dried hay, and his tan-gray eyes were like the waters of the muddy Missouri River.

Mother and Father Harper gazed at their six children, all sturdy and strong, so like the great middle western states from which they had sprung.

Tall Bill was Missouri, the Ozark State,

DOT WAS IOWA

and few states have given more in useful products to their country. Nor had many boys worked quite so hard as husky Bill. Yet Bill was also the Missouri mule, that stubborn little animal that sometimes plants its feet and will not go.

"Can't spare Bill; that's sure!" said Father Harper, looking at his oldest son. "I need him to help me in the fields."

Dot was Iowa, the Wild Rose State, "beautiful land" in the Indian language. To Iowa, long years ago, came pioneer women, bringing with them little slips and roots to plant in their western gardens; bringing faith and courage, too, and dreams of education. Today, in Iowa, a larger percentage of the population read and write than in any other state.

Dot was a lovely little angel with pigtails. Her pretty nose was buried in books whenever she was not helping her mother cook and milk and take care of children and of chickens.

"Dot's mighty handy around the house," said Mother Harper, smiling proudly at her oldest daughter. "It would be hard for me to do without her."

"Ted and Tess are too young to go," said Father Harper, with a glance at the fat little, rosy-cheeked tots. They were sitting at the table shoveling food into their

TED AND TESS

mouths like firemen stoking an engine.

The baby was Kansas. His eyes were like big sunflowers which grow so plentifully in the Sunflower State. He had soft, fair hair, like the waving fields of wheat. He was the center of his family, as Kansas is the center of the United States.

"Surely not the baby!" said Mother

Harper, as she rocked her youngest in her arms.

And now there remained but one child, and that child was David.

David was Nebraska, the Tree Planter State. It was the stage of a great drama, "The Winning of the West," in which a brave scout named Kit Carson played a leading rôle.

It saw parades of pioneers march by, and pony express riders dash headlong across the continent. A state of dreams and dreamers, of adventurers and fighters!

"Seems as if Davie should be the one to go," said Mother Harper.

David sprang to his feet and threw back his head.

"I won't go!" he cried. "I won't leave the farm, ever!"

"But we're poor, Davie," said his mother anxiously. "We're badly in need of Aunt Sophie's help."

David turned to his father.

"Please don't send me to the city, Pa!" he begged. "Please let me stay and work in the fields. I'm a-goin' to be a farmer some day. Yes, sir, I am! And I'm a-goin' to make our farm the best in these parts. See if I don't!"

"But, Davie," said Father Harper, "the land's no good. It's failed us!"

"No, Pa," answered David. "The land never fails people. Only sometimes it gets kind of scared."

"Scared?" asked Father Harper curiously. "Of what?"

"Of storms," explained David. "Dust and cyclone and such. Then, seems as if it hides its crops clear away. But now that the drought is over and we can begin to work the land, we needn't worry. Why, soon we won't need Aunt Sophie's help or anybody's help at all! Please, Pa, give the farm one more chance."

Both parents remained silent as the little

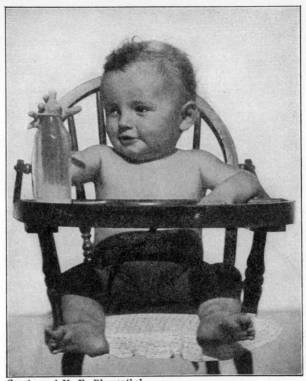

Courtesy of M. U. Blumenthal

THE BABY WAS KANSAS

boy's earnest voice rang in their ears.

At last Father Harper said, "You've sure made me feel ashamed, Davie. I've been cowardly, and no mistake. But I'm going to start raising new crops, and we'll write

Aunt Sophie that our child crop is not for sale!''

Everyone laughed except Mother Harper She looked grave.

"That's as it may be," she said. "But supposing we should have more storms, more trouble from the weather?"

"Then," said Father Harper, and he, too, became grave, "I guess we'd have to send one of you to live with Aunt Sophie. But," he added, brightening, "don't let's fret about that. The storms are over."

"The storms are over! The storms are over!" sang little Tess. "I want some apple pie."

Everybody laughed again. They were very happy now.

But somehow Dot could not help remembering the angry, black cloud she had seen that afternoon, frowning in the midst of the glowing sunset.

CHAPTER III

THE WEATHER

Omaha, Nebraska, makes more butter than any other city on earth. It has flour mills and cracker factories. It is a food center, and stout Aunt Sophie Harper looked as though she had eaten all the food.

Aunt Sophie's great, glossy automobile was sliding smoothly along the brick city streets. It stopped for the traffic light, and a newsboy jumped upon the running board, shouting, "Buy a paper, lady! Paper!"

Aunt Sophie's plump face turned a reddish purple and she screamed, "Go away! Shoo! I dislike small boys! You're a nuisance! Scat!"

Then she turned to her maid, who had not said a word. "And do not talk back to me, Martha!" she cried, shaking a finger in the

28

girl's face. "I tell you I do dislike small boys!"

Martha opened her mouth to speak, but Aunt Sophie went right on. "Why is it," she asked, "that, out of forty-five parks in Omaha, I had to be taken to one which was crawling with small boys—simply crawling?"

"But, madam," put in the maid, timidly, "I'm sure the little boy at Elmwood Park did not mean to annoy you."

"Did not mean to annoy me!" howled Aunt Sophie. "No, indeed! He only meant to destroy me. Running his bicycle over my feet, the cunning, playful little—little rattlesnake!"

She hissed loudly. "All boys are rattlesnakes! Do you hear me?"

The maid heard her. In fact, the whole street heard her.

They drove to another of Omaha's lovely parks and drew up alongside a beautiful lake.   Lumbering heavily out of her car, Aunt Sophie glanced about.

"Not a little rattlesnake in sight," she announced.

With her patient maid, she started to walk around the edge of the lake, her cane tapping in short, angry taps.   But, all at once, she stopped and pointed to a pretty little girl who was playing with a doll and buggy.

"See, Martha," she said.   "Girls are different.   They are quiet and civilized.   Now, I hope that the new child will be as pretty as that one."

Martha nodded obediently.   In her heart, however, she was pitying the child who was coming from a farm to live at Aunt Sophie's house.

Martha knew that Aunt Sophie's brother, a poor farmer, had written, asking his sister for money.   The wealthy woman had agreed to help him, providing he would let her have one of his children.

Courtesy of J. I. Case Company

FILLING THE COW'S PANTRY WITH A MODERN SILO FILLER

Aunt Sophie had not yet received an answer, yet she seemed quite certain that her brother would send her one of his little girls. How unpleasant for the child, thought Martha, if it should turn out to be a little boy!

Meanwhile, on his father's farm, David was walking home across the fields. He was looking up at a strange, dull sky. He had been out in the hot, sticky weather since daylight and he was tired.

But David was happy, too, because last night his father had promised to let him stay on at the farm. They were going to write to Aunt Sophie and refuse her offer.

David would not have to go and live in Omaha, unless, of course, more weather demons came out of the sky to discourage his father.

He looked up, just as a furious wind began to whistle across the field. It chased the clouds. It was like a band of rushing ghost figures in a hurry. It lifted the big straw hat from David's head, but he caught it just in time and jammed it down more firmly.

In the farmyard, he could see chicken feathers floating upward. His mother was taking down the washing. Her skirts blew up like a big balloon. She finished her task and started crawling along the side of the house toward the kitchen door. She was afraid of being blown away.

Everything pointed to an approaching cyclone!

More and more swiftly blew the wind until it roared about the farm, and David had all he could do to keep his balance.

Inside the kitchen, he found the family gathered in a frightened group.

Little Tess was crying, and Ted shouted, "Oh, Davie, it's a cyclone! A twister, Davie!"

The baby began to wail, and Dot lifted him out of his high chair.

David walked to the window and stood looking out. A grove of willowy trees was bowing low to the ground. It grew darker and darker, and finally there came the clatter of hail, like a million bullets, on the roof.

A cloud in the heavens formed a long, wild, licking tongue and went swirling through space.

"Quick!" cried Father Harper. "The cyclone cellar!"

They rushed out into the back yard, to an underground cave, all but David, who did not move; who still stood over by the window, watching the scene outside.

He was remembering the days when dust had been their enemy. People choking with dust. Floors and walls thick with it. Animals and trees and crops dying with it. Horrible!

And now that the dry spell was over and things were beginning to look hopeful, a cyclone had come to attack them.

Courtesy of Nebraska Farmer

A NEBRASKA CATTLE RANCH

Perhaps the farmhouse would be carried away by the wind. Such things had happened. Perhaps the crops would be beaten into the earth by hail, the land flooded, their farm destroyed.

Yet, even so, it could all be built up again —all except his father's courage. That, thought David, would now be lost forever.

A crash! A flash! Then splintered pieces of the small tool house went flying by the window. Horses were neighing wildly from the barn as the boiling pot of weather-wickedness overflowed the earth.

But gradually the wind died down, the thunder boomed a distant, parting roll, and all was over.

Yes, all was over, David told himself, as he watched his family reënter the room from the cyclone cellar.

Father Harper walked over to the window and looked out. He saw his roofless barn. He saw his fields turned into lakes, his cornstalks flat and crushed. His face was shrunken, like a fallen walnut. His shoulders were bent, his step heavy.

Then slowly he turned and made his way to the old-fashioned cupboard standing in the corner. Among the heavy, white brown-rimmed dishes, he found paper, pen and ink. He carried them to the kitchen table, and the family watched silently as he sat down and lifted up his pen.

"Well," he said. "The farm's clear washed out now, and I guess there's nothing for it but to write Aunt Sophie for help. Davie'll have to go to Omaha."

With that, he started to write in a stiff hand: "Dear Sister Sophie—"

FATHER HARPER STARTED TO WRITE

CHAPTER IV

THE SEPARATING

The letter for Aunt Sophie was clutched in David's hot little hand. His father had given it to him to mail, and now he was on his way to the nearest town.

However, down by the tall cottonwood trees he paused. He was never going to see the farm again after tomorrow. After tomorrow, he was going away to Omaha to live with a strange lady in a big city! And though he had never been to one, David felt that he would hate a big city.

"What are you doing, David?"

Dot had appeared beside him. She carried a little spade, for she had been working in the vegetable garden.

David brushed a sleeve across his eyes.

Nobody, especially Dot, should ever know how terrible he was feeling.

"I'm heading for town," he answered her, and promptly sat down upon a stone.

Dot laughed. "Seems as if you're in a big hurry," she said.

The letter to Aunt Sophie dangled from David's hand. He wanted to put off the mailing of that letter as long as he could. He threw a stone and did not reply.

"David," said Dot, moving closer to him. "You've always set such store by the farm, I was thinking we might ask Ma and Pa to send me away in your place."

David's head shot up. "Oh, Dot!" he cried. "Do you reckon they would?"

"I'm not sure," she answered. "But I'll tell them I want to study at a city school and then maybe they will."

"Oh, gosh!" David arose. "That would sure be fine!" he said. "Because, you see, Dot, I've just got to stick to the farm."

"I'M HEADING FOR TOWN," HE ANSWERED.

His eyes began to shine. "I have a notion," he went on, "that if folks work hard, they 'most always find a fortune in the ground!"

To David, that fortune meant rich, golden crops, even though the farm looked hopeless and forlorn after the storm. Trees were uprooted, fences were down, and the air was full of the odor of spoiling vegetation. But David had faith.

"Come on, Dot!" he cried. "Let's go now and ask Ma and Pa to let me stay at home!"

They started toward the house, when, all at once, David stopped and looked at his sister. Perhaps Dot was doing this just to help him. Perhaps she did not want to go to Omaha at all.

"Are—are you sure you won't mind going, Dot?" he asked.

"Not a mite!" she answered quickly. "Why, I'm going to travel further away than that some day when I'm big! I want to go clear around the United States. I've read so much about things and I want to see all of them!"

She seemed very eager. Yet David did not know that, just then, she was seeing before her tear-filled eyes the baby's pink little face; that she had to talk very fast in order not to cry.

"First," she said, "I'll visit Lincoln, Nebraska, and the fine capitol building, with the big statue of 'The Sower' on top of it. I think he's supposed to be all the Nebraska farmers who scattered seed on the plains and made things grow. Then I want to see the bones of dead animals that—"

"Bones of dead animals?" cried David. "What are you talking about?"

"They call them prehistoric fossils," said Dot.

"Mighty fancy words," smiled David. "Where are they?"

"In Nebraska's Bad Lands," answered Dot. "Huge beasts that lived clear back in the days before history began. Their bones were dug up."

"Why didn't they leave 'em be?" sniffed David. "Can't eat old bones, can you? No sense to it!"

But Dot answered that there were fine museums throughout the country where

Courtesy of J. I. Case Company

A MODERN THRESHING MACHINE

history is studied from just such fossils. She said that there was a museum at Arbor Lodge, with specimens of every kind of Nebraska tree.

When they reached the farmhouse, they waited until Father Harper returned from the fields. Then they told him their plan.

"I don't want to go to Aunt Sophie, Pa," said David. "And Dot's pining to see dead animals, so—"

"Land sakes!" gasped Mother Harper. "Whatever ails you two?"

"No, Davie," said Father Harper kindly. "Dot will have to stay. Your ma needs her to help in the house."

"Besides," added Mother Harper, setting the kettle on the stove, "Dot's very good at selling the eggs and butter and soon she'll be making a fair income for us."

"But I can do that, Ma!" pleaded David. "I can do all of Dot's work!"

"Sufferin' snakes, Dave!" laughed Bill,

"I'M GOING TO STICK TO THE FARM."

who had just come in from the barn. "You'd sure look comical mendin' socks!"

David glared at him. "No more comical than pourin' tea in Aunt Sophie's la-de-da parlor, I guess! Aw, shucks!" And he kicked the floor savagely with his clumsy boot.

"Please, Ma," begged Dot. "Let me go instead. I'd like to be a great lady and pour tea, and—and maybe some day I could even be a teacher."

Dot knew that this would make her mother think. And it did. Mother Harper thought a thousand thoughts. She looked at Dot, so gentle and pretty—just the sort of child for a wealthy lady in a splendid home like Aunt Sophie's.

Then she looked at David, twisting his hardened hands together, a frown on his sun-toughened, freckled face. Grubby little David!

"I declare!" said Mother Harper finally. "The girl is right!"

So, two days later, Father Harper drove up to the door in the old Ford car. He was going to take Dot to the station. He had written Aunt Sophie to expect her.

The family stood awkwardly about, Mother Harper wiping her eyes with the corner of her apron. She handed Dot a basket of lunch, to be eaten on the train. Nobody knew just how to act or just what to say.

Big Bill whittled a stick, pretending not to care. Ted and Tess clutched their mother's skirt and their mouths twitched at the corners. Even the baby, usually so bright, whimpered fretfully.

A lump came into David's throat, and he wished with all his might that he could run away and hide. Dot tried to smile as she kissed each one good-bye. But when she came to the baby, she could not keep back the tears any longer and broke down weeping.

"Let's get on our way!" called Father Harper, from outside. "Mighty little time left, and trains don't wait for folks!"

At last they were gone, and David stood watching the battered old car rattling its way down the road. When Dot's waving handkerchief was a tiny speck in the distance, he turned and went over to the barn.

He tried to forget that he would not see Dot again for a long time, maybe never. He tried to forget, too, how bitterly she had cried before going away.

An old brown cow came up to the fence and sniffed in a friendly way. He stroked her, and suddenly his head dropped down upon her soft, smooth neck.

" 'Tain't right! No, 'tain't!" he sobbed. "Not a one of us should ever leave the farm —ever!"

A frightened voice was calling his name. He looked up and saw Bill running toward him from the house.

"Come quick, Davie! There's been an accident!" he gasped. "I'm headin' for Thompson's to phone the doctor."

Before David could say a word, his brother was gone.

An accident, Bill had said! What sort of accident? Who was hurt?

Swiftly he ran toward the house, his

"T'AIN'T RIGHT! NO T'AIN'T!"

heart hammering within him. He found the entire family, with the exception of Bill, in the parlor. The parlor! Why, that room was only used when the minister called!

Mother Harper was bending over the sofa; her eyes were red with crying. Father Harper stood silently in a corner, the picture of distress; the children huddled together in a frightened group. David saw Dot lying still and pale upon the sofa, and then he knew.

"Pa—he had an accident with the—the automobile," sobbed Mother Harper, as David remained standing in the doorway. "Oh, Davie, come here," she continued, "for Dot's been badly hurt and she's asking for you! Merciful Heavens, if the doctor would only get here!"

Dot badly hurt! David could hardly believe it. Why, only a short time ago she had been waving him good-bye.

The doctor came at last. When he finally

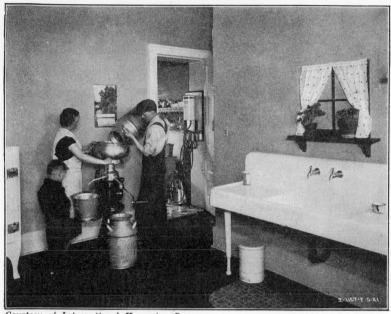

Courtesy of International Harvester Company

A MODERN CREAM SEPARATOR

went away, he left behind him a broken-hearted little family. It would be a long time before Dot would ever walk again. Her back had been injured.

"She must have great care and special treatment," he said, as he took his leave, "or she may never get well at all."

Just how poor Father Harper was going

to manage this without any money was the
question.   But the doctor did not ask; it was
not his place to know the answer.

The family did know an answer, however,
and that answer was Aunt Sophie.   Now,
even more than before, they must send Aunt
Sophie one of the children.   And since Dot
could not go, David must.

Poor little David!   "I want to stick to the
farm," he had said.   "I have a notion that if
folks work hard, they 'most always find a
fortune in the ground."

But David did not know, and neither did
anyone else, that a fortune really did lie underground—a fortune in hard, gold nuggets!

CHAPTER V

THE UPROOTING

Aunt Sophie watched the train as it roared into the station. She smiled in a satisfied sort of way because she thought that her new little daughter was on that train.

As the passengers began to alight, Aunt Sophie's round eyes searched the crowd. But she saw no little girl.

When everyone else had gone, however, an awkward, blond little boy stood alone upon the platform. He carried a lunch basket over one arm and clutched a miserable-looking suitcase under the other.

His trousers were too large for him and his coat was too small. He was gazing about in a half-startled, half-excited way. For David Harper had never, in the whole of his life, seen anything so splendid as Omaha's Union Pacific Station.

Dot had once told him that Omaha is the fourth railroad center in the United States. She had said that Abraham Lincoln made it the starting point for the first transcontinental railroad.

But David had not realized how big and grand it would be. He could have stood there, watching those fierce, black engines all day long. But suddenly he remembered that he must find Aunt Sophie.

His father had described Aunt Sophie to him as a stout lady, with a very haughty manner. Why, there she was!

He walked up to her and introduced himself. Then he explained about Dot's unfortunate accident and how he had been sent in her place.

"Heavens above!" gasped Aunt Sophie. She looked at David as though he were some unknown creature out of a zoo. "Were you

Courtesy of The Omaha World-Herald

UNION STATION, OMAHA, NEBRASKA

the next best they had?   Dear me, how pain-
ful!"

But a young lady who was with Aunt
Sophie smiled and said, "Come along, David.
I'll take your suitcase."

All the way home in the car, Aunt Sophie
muttered things to herself.   David frequently caught the words, "small boys" and
"little rattlesnakes."

The other lady, whose name was Martha,

talked to him pleasantly, however. She pointed out shops and theatres, great buildings so tall that David wondered why they did not topple over. He could not understand why the automobiles did not hit one another as they whizzed along the streets.

Aunt Sophie's house was set in a most magnificent garden, with trees and lakes. It was all like something Dot used to read about. It did not seem real to David.

But Aunt Sophie did seem real. Very real indeed! When she scolded, her voice was like a thunderbolt, and she scolded constantly.

"Bathe him and have his hair cut," she commanded Martha as soon as they had arrived at home. "Then dress him in clean clothes—and keep him away from me!"

David thought this would not be so great a punishment for him. He felt rather relieved that he would not have to see very much of Aunt Sophie!

But in the next few weeks David was to find his life one long punishment! He hated city clothes. He missed his overalls and old straw hat.

At school, the boys teased him because he talked like a farmer and could not play their games. They called him "Hayseed" and "Corn Tassel."

Aunt Sophie sent him to school every day in the automobile, though the distance was not great. Aunt Sophie wanted her neighbors to believe that she was doing a great, good deed for a poor little farm boy. She wanted them to say that she was kind and charitable.

David begged to be permitted to walk to school, but Martha told him that he must obey Aunt Sophie's orders. Everybody always obeyed Aunt Sophie's orders.

When he reached home in the afternoons, he had to take a bath and then remain cooped up in his room until supper time. He

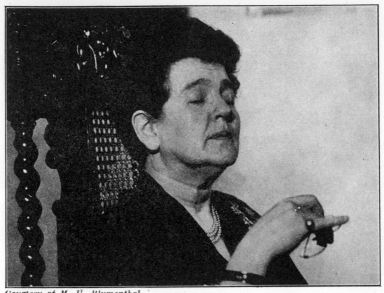

AUNT SOPHIE

had no friends and no one with whom to talk, except Martha.   Worst of all, he was never allowed out in the open air, which he loved so well.

He tried not to think of the farm and of the family—of those cheerful faces about the supper table each evening.   But his head began to feel stuffy and queer and he longed for the sun and the wind.

His legs wanted to move and his arms to swing. They were legs and arms that had grown strong and brown with exercising in the fields.

And so it happened that, one evening, when Martha came into his room with his supper tray, David was not there. Martha searched for him all over the house, but he was gone.

Trembling, the poor maid was finally forced to tell Aunt Sophie. Aunt Sophie almost jumped out of her chair.

"What!" she bellowed. "The rascal is gone? He's dared to run away from me? Oh, what a disgrace! What will people say? Go find him at once and bring him back! Do you hear me!"

But just then David walked into the room! His cheeks were pink and his hair was tousled.

"I didn't run away," he said.

He stood before Aunt Sophie's chair, very

straight, with his head thrown back. "I just got tired of sittin' indoors all the time, and I wanted to do some walking. So I went out."

"W-ent out?" gobbled Aunt Sophie. "Where did you go?"

"To the stockyards," answered David.

"The s-stockyards!" Aunt Sophie hissed and rolled her eyes. "Whatever possessed you to go to a horrible, smelly place like that?"

Aunt Sophie did not bother to recall that it was this same "smelly" place where her husband had made his money. He was dead now, but he had been a commission man who traded in cattle. For Omaha is the third largest livestock market in the United States.

"Well, you see, ma'am," answered David, "I'm mighty keen about such things because I plan to be a farmer some day."

"A farmer!" screamed Aunt Sophie. "What a dreadful idea! You are certainly

STOCK YARDS, OMAHA, NEBRASKA

not going to be a farmer! You are my son now. You must live in the city—always! Do you hear?"

David remembered the cattle, the hogs and sheep he had seen herded into pens at the stockyards. They had been sent in from farms to be sold. The only difference between them and himself seemed that he would not be made into beefsteak, ham or lamb chops.

But then, neither was he going to permit Aunt Sophie to make him into a city man!

"I'm a-goin' to be a farmer," he repeated, firmly. "And nobody can stop me!"

Aunt Sophie blew up like a burst balloon. "You are not!" she thundered. "And, if you ever try to go out again alone, I shall write to your family!"

"I'll write to them myself!" cried David hotly, and he dashed out of the room.

When he had left, Aunt Sophie turned to her maid.

"Bring me the letter he writes before it is mailed," she said. "And if the little gopher has said anything against me, why—"

"What will you do to him, madam?" quavered Martha.

"I'll—I'll—" Aunt Sophie hesitated, trying to think of some punishment severe enough. Then, suddenly she laughed. "Why, I'll send the grubby little tiger to school in petticoats! That's what I'll do to him!"

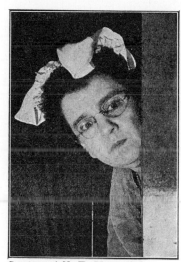

Courtesy of M. U. Blumenthal

A HEAD SHOT OUT

CHAPTER VI

CULTIVATING

When David reached his room that evening he decided not to write a letter to his family. They were helpless to do anything for him. And besides, why worry them? Furthermore, he had a feeling that if he set down on paper his angry thoughts, he would later be sorry for it.

And David was right. Every day Aunt Sophie asked Martha whether the boy had written, and every day Martha answered that he had not.

"Well, when he does," rumbled Aunt Sophie, "I want to read the letter to see whether he has said anything horrid about me in it. I'm sure he will. So, remember: Bring it directly to me."

Poor Martha had to promise, and, at last one evening, David did begin a letter. It was to his sister Dot.

"DEAR DOT," he wrote, "*There is a King of Omaha! And a Queen, too! I guess you'll hardly believe me, but I went to the palace last night and saw them.*

"*Oh, but it sure was a fine sight! All fixed up with flowers and ribbons, and there were Dukes and Knights and Princes dancing around. There was a parade, too, and I was one of the pages. We carried the Queen's train.*

"*Of course there was no sense to my clothes and I felt like a monkey in them. But everybody was dressed up fancy, and it was all right pretty. I declare, I was feeling sort of proud, when something happened. Something awful, Dot!*

"*Well, we were coming down the steps from the golden throne, and all of a sudden,*

I heard a tearing noise.   Then, up went my feet in the air, and down I went, sliding the whole staircase till I hit the bottom!

"Dot, I'd stepped smack on the Queen's train and been toppled upside down!

"Well, sir, everyone was laughing fit to kill, but Aunt Sophie got boiling mad!   She said she was mortified.   You see, Aunt Sophie sets so much store by things like that and she's always getting mortified.

"I declare, she sure is a silly, sour old turnip!   But then, I guess I'll get along here all right.   So don't any of you back home fret about me.   How are the crops?

Your loving brother,

DAVID."

David looked up and noticed that Martha had entered the room.

"Let me take your letter, David," she said. "I—I'll mail it for you."   But she did not look at him as she spoke.   She was ashamed

because she was going to give the letter to
Aunt Sophie.

"That's very nice of you, Martha," said
David, and started to lick the envelope
closed.

"I heard what happened to you at the ball
last night," went on Martha, "and I'm sorry,
David. But," she added, smiling, "I'm sure
the King and Queen did not mind it one bit!"

David smiled back gratefully. "Well,
gosh," he said, "that's sure kind of 'em!
I've always heard that royal folks are kind
and generous."

"Why, David," she said, "I really think
you believe that they were an honest-to-
goodness King and Queen!"

"Well, say, weren't they?" asked David,
wide-eyed.

"Of course not, David!" laughed Martha.
"They were two popular citizens of Omaha
dressed up like royalty for the Ak-sar-ben
Ball!"

Courtesy of Knights of Ak-Sar-Ben

AN AK-SAR-BEN HARVEST CELEBRATION IN OMAHA.

"What is Ak-sar-ben?" inquired David.

"Spell it backwards and find out," said Martha.

David did, and was amazed to discover that it spelled another word—the name of his state.

"Ak-sar-ben is a booster organization," explained Martha, "That means that its members do all they can to bring Nebraska to the attention of the world.   Besides the yearly ball, they hold horse races and a live-stock show."

"Well, sufferin' toads!" cried David.   "Did you ever?   And me writing to Dot that I was at a real palace!"

"That was the Ak-sar-ben Coliseum," said Martha.   "And now," she added, "give me your letter, David, and go to bed.   It's getting late."

She reached out her hand for the letter, but David held it back and shook his head.

"No," he said.   "I'll have to open it again

Courtesy of Knights of Ak-Sar-Ben
"BILLY," 1936 GRAND CHAMPION OF THE AK-SAR-BEN
4-H BABY BEEF SHOW

and tell Dot what you just told me about the
Ak-sar-ben. She'll sure like that. She's always interested in those things!"

Martha laughed. "Very well, David," she
said. "I'll get the letter in the morning.
Now, sleep well."

David did sleep well. He dreamed that
Aunt Sophie was Queen of the Ak-sar-ben

Ball and he was carrying her train. Only they were standing by the pig pen on his father's farm, and he stepped on her train and Aunt Sophie went splashing into the pig pen!

Yes, David slept very well! And when he awoke it was early in the morning, but the sun poured into his room. What a day to go for a walk!

Perhaps he could slip out for just a few minutes before breakfast and before Aunt Sophie was awake. He would take along his letter to Dot and mail it, saving Martha the trouble.

He jumped out of bed and dressed. Then he stuffed the letter into his pocket, opened the bedroom door and started to tiptoe down the hallway. He had to pass Aunt Sophie's door, so he was extra careful not to make a noise.

If Aunt Sophie knew about this, she would be furious. She would be afraid that the neighbors might see him and say that she was not taking good care of him. Silly, sour Aunt Sophie!

David chuckled to himself, remembering that he had used those very words in his letter to Dot. He had even called her a turnip!

"Perhaps," he thought, "I'm rude and ungrateful to talk like that! But, land sakes! I don't mean any harm. I'm really sorry for Aunt Sophie. She just hasn't the least idea how to be happy!"

"Where are you going, young man?"

A door had flown open and a head shot out—a head with Aunt Sophie's red face beneath a lace boudoir cap. It had the dreadful effect of a huge beet with a hat on it!

"Stop this instant! Come back here!"

David obeyed and approached her.

"What do you mean by leaving your room before Martha comes to fetch you?" she demanded.

And before David could answer, she put her hand quickly into his pocket and snatched out his letter to Dot.

"Ah, this is just what I thought!" she cried. "So you were trying to sneak away to mail it! You didn't want me to know what you wrote about me, eh? Well, I shall soon find out! Now, go back to your room until I send for you!"

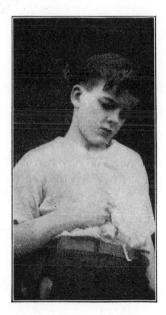

CHAPTER VII

THE SLIPPING

"I won't, I tell you! I won't!" screamed David. "You can't make me—ever!"

He stood white-faced and furious before Aunt Sophie, who pointed to a girl's dress and bonnet which she had laid out upon his bed.

"Indeed you will!" she answered. "You'll wear them to school today. I'll teach you to write to your family and call me names!"

"You can't make me wear girl's clothes! You can't!" repeated David hoarsely.

"Besides," went on Aunt Sophie, as though she had not heard him, "besides, I wanted a girl in the first place, so I shall dress you as one! Now, put on the clothes!"

"No! No! Never!" David shook his

Courtesy of Knights of Ak-Sar-Ben

BOYS AND GIRLS OF THE 4-H CLUBS WITH THEIR ENTRIES
AT THE ANNUAL AK-SAR-BEN LIVE STOCK AND HORSE SHOW.

head and planted his back against the wall;
his eyes were flashing.

"Do as I say," commanded Aunt Sophie,
"and come to me when you are dressed!"

With that she left the room and closed the
door behind her.

But Aunt Sophie had not meant to send
David to school in skirts. She would never
have done such a thing because she feared

her neighbors' tongues far too much. She had only wanted to frighten the boy and also to try his pluck.

"He's like all the Harpers," she told herself now, as she went to her room. "Full of pepper! Well, we'll just see what he expects to do about this!"

What David was doing would have amazed Aunt Sophie. He was not putting on the girl's dress. Instead, he had pulled out his faded, farm overalls from the old, basket suitcase where they had been packed away.

He quickly slipped them on, packed the few belongings he had brought with him from home, and closed the suitcase again. He was going to run away! He was going back to the farm! And nobody, not even Aunt Sophie, could stop him!

He opened the door of his room and ran on tiptoe, through the long hallway to the staircase. He slid noiselessly down the slippery, shiny banisters to the floor below, carefully opened the heavy front door and made his way out of Aunt Sophie's house.

Anger still burned in his heart and there was but one thought in his mind.   Home! Home to the farm!

The postman passed him as he scurried along the shady walk to the front gate.   The postman carried a letter addressed to "David Harper the Third."

But David Harper the Third, ran blindly on, out into the street, away from Aunt Sophie's house, away from the city!   Back to the farm!

CHAPTER VIII

THE HOMESTEAD

The city of Omaha started to grow from
the days of the western gold rush. At that
time, a ferry was built to cross the Missouri
River. It was built for travelers, on their
way to free lands. And today, through the
modern streets of Omaha, ran another trav-
eler, making his way toward freedom!

As David pushed on, the word, "Home!
Home!" echoed in his ears. Then, suddenly,
he caught the sound of other words—words
that made him turn cold all over.

"Extra!" newsboys were calling. "Read
all about the big floods! Nebraska farms
destroyed! Extra! Extra!"

David stopped in the middle of the street
and an enormous truck came within an inch

of running him down. The driver swerved quickly and called David an unflattering name.

But David had not even noticed. He was walking along again and now his face was white for he was filled with a new fear. Floods had destroyed Nebraska farms! Perhaps his father's farm had been among them!

He bought a newspaper and hurried on until he reached the railway station. Fortunately, he still had the money his father had given him the day he left home.

Seated in a train, he began to read about the floods. They had indeed swept away whole homesteads in the very valley where his family lived.

David gritted his teeth. So those wicked weather-children, tired of flying kites, had been using the land as a pond to sail their boats on!

Well, David would show them some day

Courtesy of J. I. Case Company

CULTIVATING ACRES OF CORN IN IOWA

that man can conquer all the wind and frost
and flood that ever blew or bit or drowned!

But when David alighted from the train
at the familiar little town near his farm, a
sad sight met his eyes. Roofless houses
stood like the scalped victims of Indian raids.
Highways, once so smooth and white, were

washed away, and trees stretched broken limbs to a dull, gray sky.

There were ugly water puddles everywhere and David, walking toward home, was soon splattered from head to foot with mud.

As he neared the farm, his heart beat in quick, jumping thumps and he wondered what he was about to find there. Some of the houses along the way had been completely destroyed, others only partly, while a few still stood their ground.

David had not stopped in the town to ask questions; he had preferred to discover the truth for himself. And now, as he rounded the bend in the road, where his father's windmill had always flashed a greeting to him, he did, at last, find out what he had dreaded to know.

There was no more windmill! No house, no barn, no silo! Nothing left! Nothing except soaked land and a few shivering trees.

A thrill of horror shook David. He shuddered, turned, and ran as fast as he could to the neighboring farm.

The Thompsons' house still stood! David breathed a sigh of relief.

Mrs. Thompson met him at the door and answered his burning questions. Yes, his family had been rescued after a most dreadful experience. And Father Harper had moved them all to St. Louis, where he expected to find work as a laborer.

"Anything," Father Harper had said, "is better than what I have put up with on the farm. This is the end of my patience with the weather, and no mistake!"

But, even as David looked around him at the dreary, flood-wrecked country, it was not the end for him. The land was still there.

"I declare, Davie Harper," said Mrs. Thompson, "you do look poorly! I expect what you need's a good, hot meal. Now, come along inside, for we're just fixin' to have supper."

Courtesy of Chicago and North Western Ry. Company

A NEBRASKA WHEAT FARM

After supper, when Farmer Thompson sat smoking his pipe by the stove, David told them his story. When he had finished, the two good people did not speak, and David stood looking out of the window at the dusk.

"Well, Davie," at last drawled Farmer Thompson. "I reckon you'll be wantin' to head toward St. Louis and your folks right away. Likely tomorrow. But you're welcome to stay here with us overnight."

"I'm much obliged, sir," said David. "And it's mighty kind of you. But, if you don't mind, I won't!"

"You won't stay?" asked Farmer Thompson. He raised his bushy eyebrows.

"No, sir," said David. "Not only tonight —but all the time! You see, I'd like to stay with you for keeps, if you'll have me!"

"Well, bless my soul!" cried Mrs. Thompson, turning from her dishes and wiping her hands on her apron. "Whatever are you sayin', David Harper? Your family will be wantin' you in St. Louis as soon's ever they hear you've left your auntie's house in Omaha!"

"But I won't go to St. Louis," said David, "or to any city—ever again! I'm staying right on here and working for you on your farm, Mr. Thompson, if you'll let me pay my board and keep that way. Will you, sir?"

Farmer Thompson had only one son, who had gone to the city not so long ago. So Farmer Thompson was sorely in need of help, and the idea of a boy like David to do the chores appealed to him. He smiled.

"Why, sure, Davie," he said, removing the pipe slowly from his mouth. "I expect I can use you around here. And, likely, your pa'll be glad of one less mouth to feed while he's trying to break soil in the city."

"There's no soil in the city," said David, bitterly. "Only hard stone and dirt and— and meanness!"

At the recollection of Aunt Sophie's treatment, tears choked him and he turned abruptly from the window and dashed out of the house.

Not until he reached his father's farm did he stop, and then only when he came to the clump of cottonwood trees where his grandfather's cabin had once stood.

"It's still our farm," he thought doggedly, brushing the tears out of his eyes, "even if it is clear washed out now. But I'm stayin' at Thompson's so I can come over here every day and work it! I'm a-goin' to raise crops out of this old ground yet! See if I don't!"

He kicked the soil and did not know that he was kicking at the very earth which covered a fortune in gold!

CHAPTER IX

THE TRANSPLANTING

Dot Harper sat in an easy chair by the window and looked down upon the narrow, noisy street. Dot could not go out, and often, as today, she was left alone in the flat. Her mother had gone marketing and taken the baby along. The other children were in school.

As she watched the milling crowds below, Dot played a game. She had read that in olden days St. Louis was a French fur-trading colony. It was very gay and colorful.

Today, it is the principal city in the State of Missouri, the most important city west of the Mississippi River. It leads the world in the making and selling of various articles, and Dot's game was to see how many of

Courtesy of St. Louis Chamber of Commerce
POLAR BEARS IN THE ST. LOUIS ZOO

these interesting articles she could count.

They passed so quickly that it made her dizzy. Hats, furs, bags, shoes. Every fifth man in the nation is supposed to be wearing a pair of St. Louis shoes!

The clang, clang of street cars brought to Dot's mind the fact that St. Louis sends street cars to every country in the world.

A wonderful city, she thought! All earnest business, and the closest of any other to the great farms of the Middle West.

But in remembering the farm, Dot had also remembered the flood! She shuddered, and leaned back in her chair, trying to forget. Instead, she fell into a troubled sleep, and as she dreamed, the whole dreadful experience came back to her.

It was very early in the morning and she was hearing the strange swish, swish of water outside her door. She was hearing Father Harper's voice shouting:

"Get up! Get up! The yard's full of water! It's coming into the house!"

A thin stream had begun to trickle under her door, and soon the water was creeping over the floors, like slippery, silvery snakes.

Terrified, the family had climbed up the rickety, old stairs to a low-ceilinged attic room, high off the ground. From the window, they could look down and watch their farm being turned into a lake. A hencoop floated in the yard and on it sat a screaming chicken.

Courtesy of Hannibal Chamber of Commerce

MARK TWAIN STANDING IN FRONT OF HIS BOYHOOD
HOME IN HANNIBAL, MISSOURI

"The water's rising," Father Harper said.

He paced back and forth, the others watching him, too frightened to move. Mother Harper held the sleeping baby in her arms, while Ted and Tess clung tightly to her skirts. Bill had carried Dot to a rocking chair and covered her shoulders with a shawl.

Before long, tiny tongues of the flood-beast began to lick their way even into the

attic, so the family clambered upon the roof.
Rain was heavily falling out of leaden skies
and they shivered, huddled miserably together.

Little Tess began to cry, and Dot reached
out her hand to draw the child toward her.
But the roof was so slippery that she found
herself sliding. Panic-stricken, she gripped
with all her might to keep from falling off.

"Pa, oh, Pa!" screamed Ted. "The house
is moving! I'm scared! I'm scared!"

There was a creaking of boards and a horrible, swaying motion.

"Hold on for your lives!" cried Father
Harper.

With a final wrench, the house broke loose
and started to plunge about in the angry water, like a ship-wrecked barrel. For hours
it seemed, they were tossed here and there,
clinging to one another, expecting, at any
moment, to be dashed to pieces. Then, suddenly, out of the storm they saw a raft ap-

proaching.   There were three men upon it.

"Save us!   Save us!"

"Wake up, Dottie!   Land sakes!"

Mother Harper had come home and was bending above Dot.

"Forevermore, child!" she exclaimed. "Whatever are you screaming about?"

Dot opened her eyes to find that she was not out on the roof of a flood-wrecked house. She was not wet and cold and in danger, but safe at home in their city flat.

Smiling gratefully up at Mother Harper, Dot told her what she had been dreaming. But Mother Harper looked at the little girl with grave concern in her eyes.

Dot's cheeks were too rosy, her eyes too bright.   She had been worse since the flood and was growing steadily weaker.   The city doctor had ordered costly medicines and treatment.

But Dot had not received those medicines, nor the treatment, either, because Father

Harper could not afford to buy them for her.

Father Harper worked as a day laborer at the docks. Today, as the sun was going down, he stood on those docks, looking at the Mississippi River, the greatest on the continent.

He stood watching busy men unloading products from far places. Dollars and dollars and dollars pouring into this city of world trade, yet for Father Harper, nothing but poverty!

His shoulders drooped wearily as he made his way homeward. How could he tell his family what had happened to him today?

Mother Harper met him with a worry of her own. It was the worry about Dot.

"Something's just got to be done for the child," she said. "It seems as if every day she grows weaker."

Father Harper did not look at her as he replied huskily, "I'm afraid there's nothing we can do. I lost my job today."

Courtesy of Hannibal Chamber of Commerce

TOM SAWYER AND HUCK FINN MONUMENT
IN HANNIBAL, MISSOURI

For a moment tragic silence filled the room. Then Mother Harper pursed her lips tightly together and a determined look came into her face.

"There's one thing we can do," she said. "We can write to Aunt Sophie again. She must help us!"

"But you know right well she won't," said Father Harper. "Aunt Sophie's mighty angry since Davie ran away."

Mother Harper bit her lip and thought hard for a moment. Then she said:

"I've a notion she would, though, if Davie'd go back to her. Leastways, her letter showed plainly enough that she wants him."

"But, Ma," said Father Harper, "Davie doesn't want to go!"

"I've no doubt of that, Pa," replied Mother Harper. "But if it means Aunt Sophie will send us money, then he'll just have to!"

"No! No! Please!" Dot had been listening to the conversation, and now she cried out in distress. "Please don't send Davie back to the city! He'd—he'd die! I know he would! Oh, I'd rather not get well as long as I live than have Davie sent to Aunt Sophie's again! Truly I would!"

Dot was crying bitterly. Mother Harper went over and patted her shoulder.

"There, there, darling," she soothed. "Don't fret. Why, Davie won't care a mite, specially when he knows it's for your sake."

"Oh, but that's just why I can't let him do it, Ma!" sobbed Dot. "Don't you understand? He—he wrote to me and told me how he hated the city, how unhappy he was there. And now he's happy back on the farm. Please let him stay there! Promise me you won't ever take him away again!"

Father and Mother Harper looked at each other in a bewildered sort of way. What could they do? They must raise money. And yet Dot was right; it was not fair to make David go back to Omaha if he did not want to.

"We might be lucky and find someone to buy the farm," suggested Mother Harper, thinking hard.

"Someone who isn't afraid of trouble," added Father Harper grimly.

But nevertheless, Father Harper decided to go about trying to sell the farm, early tomorrow morning.

CHAPTER X

THE COUNTY FAIR

David was busy on the Thompson farm. Yet frequently he found time to walk over to his father's deserted farm, for he was planning to do many things there.

Already he had started to clear away some of the wreckage left by the flood. He dreamed of bringing new life to the old place; of surprising his father by some day raising fine, strong crops.

Farmer Thompson had promised to help him, but just now, there was much work to be done on his own farm.

David arose at dawn and milked the cows. He fed the hogs, and when they fell ill with a terrible sickness, he helped the farmer to save their lives.

The flood had not only drowned and destroyed, but it had left disease throughout the country. Land buried so long under water began to smell of dead animals and decayed plants.

In spite of all this trouble, Farmer Thompson was preparing as usual for the County Fair. As if nothing had happened, he was getting ready for that great event.

Never had a year gone by that Farmer Thompson had not shown his livestock. And never had his wife missed baking her cakes and pies and taking them, along with her spicy pickles and jellies, to the Fair.

David, too, fell into the spirit and eagerly made preparations of his own. The university was offering a prize to boys and girls for the biggest ears of corn, the finest chickens or calves.

David's pride and joy was a calf named Blackie, which he had raised himself. And now Farmer Thompson was allowing

Courtesy of J. I. Case Company

PLOWING IN IOWA WITH A MODERN TRACTOR

him to exhibit the little creature at the Fair. It made David feel as excited as the father of a small boy who is going to speak a piece at a party!

The morning of the Fair he awoke and stretched to the sweet tune of hens cackling and of roosters crowing to one another from miles apart.

David jumped out of bed and reached for his overalls. Straw fell out of them. It smelled good—so good and clean. And, through the window, he could see that the sky was blue with pink streaks where the lazy sun was trying to get up.

Already Mrs. Thompson had begun her morning pot-and-kettle-clatter in the kitchen. There would be oatmeal and milk, and thick slices of bread and fried potatoes and coffee for breakfast.

Today, at the Fair, they would sell ice cream and fancy candy in striped bags. Perhaps Blackie would win a blue ribbon—a first prize!   Perhaps?   He'd sure better!

David whistled a popular tune that he had heard on Farmer Thompson's radio, and went out into the yard.   After he had finished his chores, he began to shine Blackie's small hoofs with shoe polish. Then he rubbed the sleek, fat body and even tied a ribbon in the calf's tail.

Farmer Thompson rubbed the horns of his cows with a file and then with emery.   He polished them so that they shone, and their switches, or tails, were fluffy from having been put up in braids.

Some day David was going to have cattle like that—beautiful, well-kept cattle—some day, when he and his family were back on their own farm.

Yes, sir, he would have the best stock in the whole country, some day!   Because it did not occur to David that he might never go back to the farm again; that his father might sell the land.   Why, that land belonged to them; it had been theirs for generations!

A county fair was a pretty sight, thought David, as they arrived in the town. Bunting decorated the lamp-posts, a band played music on a platform, and there were merry-go-rounds and shooting galleries and horse races.

Mrs. Thompson spent most of the day inside a big, wooden building. Here the women displayed all kinds of sewing, embroidery, and, of course, food.

Mrs. Thompson won a prize for her plum jelly and her cheeks turned just as red as the jelly with pleasure and pride.

David helped Farmer Thompson with the cattle. They put them into pens in the live-stock building. David had quite a time trying to calm young Blackie, who seemed frightened and nervous.

David's blood raced with excitement when the final moment arrived for the giving out of the children's prizes. He thought that the judges would never finish looking over his Blackie and whispering together.

But at last one of them pinned a ribbon on the little animal's halter, and David's heart nearly broke right through his shirt. It was a blue ribbon! Blackie had won a first prize!

Farmer Thompson grinned and gripped David's hand. "I'm proud of you, Davie," he said. "You're a-goin' to make a first rate farmer. And, just to show you I'm mindful of your good work on the farm, I'm a-goin' to give you Blackie for your own!"

Blackie for his own! What a wonderful day! First, the prize; then Farmer Thompson's praise; and now, as if that hadn't been enough, Blackie for his own! The crowds passed before David in a sort of golden haze of happiness.

"See those two men standing by the hog pen yonder?" asked Farmer Thompson, pointing.

Courtesy of Jefferson City Chamber of Commerce

THE BAGNELL DAM, JEFFERSON CITY, MISSOURI

"Yes, sir," answered David. "They look like city folks."

"Yes, they are," said Farmer Thompson. "They've come all the way from St. Louis to buy up land cheap, and seems like they're aimin' to buy your pa's farm!"

Suddenly the sun went out of the sky and a black cloud covered David's world. Nothing mattered any more! Nothing at all! Not even Farmer Thompson's praise, or

Blackie's prize, or the fact that Blackie belonged to him now!   Nothing!

The farm was going to be sold!

Soon they started for home.   The highway was crowded with automobiles, many from neighboring states.   Farmer Thompson pointed to one.

"Look there," he said.   "Those folks are from Iowa, the state that gives more corn, more hogs, more eggs and more poultry than any other state."

"I thought 'twas Nebraska did that!" said Mrs. Thompson.   She was very proud of her own state.

"No, but Nebraska's got the largest butter factories," answered her husband, "and that's because our Platte Valley's the most fertile."

"Where does that auto come from?" asked Mrs. Thompson, as another car with an out-of-state license plate passed them.

"From Missouri, 'the Gateway to the

West,' " replied Farmer Thompson. "And a busy place, too! Plumb full of factories and railroads, rich mines and farms. Land sakes!" he added, laughing. "Just look at Kansas scootin' by! There's a state with mighty fine crops and cattle and meat-packing plants, too! Yes, sir, we have plenty to be proud of here in the Middle West!"

But David was not listening. The colors of the passing license plates were swimming before his tear-filled eyes. He was not even interested in hearing Farmer Thompson tell about the country he loved. He was only thinking of the terrible thing he had heard. His father's farm was going to be sold.

CHAPTER XI

THE SOWER OF DREAMS

The Harper family lived in a poor neighborhood of St. Louis and from the window of their flat, they could see the Mississippi. Dot had been reading "Tom Sawyer," and she felt as though she knew this great river as a friend.

Father Harper had not yet heard from the two men who had gone to Nebraska to look over farmlands. He did not yet know whether they were going to buy his farm. He waited impatiently for their return to St. Louis to find out.

"If they'll only see fit to buy it," he said to his wife one morning, "we'll have enough money to clear out of here and go to Kansas City."

THE LOG CABIN HOME WHICH ULYSSES S. GRANT BUILT
WITH HIS OWN HANDS.

Mother Harper was pouring the breakfast
coffee, and now she stopped with the pot held
in mid-air.

"Why should we go to Kansas City?" she
asked.

"Because," answered Father Harper, "it
is a great livestock and grain market, an important transportation city, and almost in
the center of the United States. Why, I'm
sure to find work there!"

Courtesy of Topeka Chamber of Commerce

KANSAS STATE CAPITOL, TOPEKA, KANSAS

Every place always looked better to Father Harper than the place where he happened to be at the moment. His eyes were the kind that saw greener pastures ahead.

"Furthermore," he continued, "Kansas City has some of the finest parks in the world. I guess you young ones would like that, eh?"

He glanced at his wife for approval of this last remark. Then he turned again to the children, as if he were going to tell them a story. "And what do you think?" he said. "Right across from the big railroad station, is a soldiers' memorial with a fire burning on top of it all the time!"

"Doesn't it ever go out?" asked Tess.

"Never," said Father Harper. "For it's to show that the people of Kansas City will never forget the brave soldiers who fought in the Great War."

"I'd like to see that!" whispered Dot.

"And you will," said Father Harper.

"That is if we sell the farm, for then we'll move to Kansas City, and no mistake!"

But many days went by and still the two men did not return from Nebraska. In those days Father Harper seemed to change his mind quite frequently about where he wished to live.

One evening he came home, saying that he had met a friend from Des Moines, Iowa. He now felt that this was a city where he could really be successful!

"Why, there's hundreds of factories in Des Moines," he beamed. "And big publishing houses, too, where important farm journals are printed. I'd do real well in some such business, I'm sure!"

The family listened while he went on to tell them that Des Moines is the capital and largest city of Iowa, and that it is in the midst of the great corn country.

He was very much excited about Des Moines until the next week, when he heard

Courtesy of Kansas City Southern Ry. Company

DICKEY CLAY MANUFACTURING COMPANY,
PITTSBURG, KANSAS

about Wichita, Kansas. And then he came home equally excited about the city of Wichita.

"The largest broom market in the world!" he announced, proudly, as if he had built all the broom factories in the town. "Flour mills and packing plants, and one of the finest airports in America! Yes, sir."

Mother Harper wondered what good all this was going to do Father Harper. He could not find work in St. Louis, so why did he imagine that he could find it in some other city?

Mother Harper prayed each night for the return of those two men from Nebraska with news that they had bought the farm! And her prayers were strangely different from David's. Because David, too, was praying, but in the very opposite way.

Each evening when the work was done on Thompson's farm, and the red sun sank down in a flaming ball, David ran over to his father's land.

He ran over and stood near the old cottonwood trees, wiping his sweating face with the sleeve of his faded shirt. And he spoke in an angry whisper to his unseen enemy— those men who wanted to buy the farm.

"You leave it be!" he growled, between set teeth. "This is our farm, and I'm not goin' to give it up—ever!"

However, as the days marched along and nobody came, and Father Harper did not write, David breathed easier once again.

"Maybe they won't buy it after all," he thought, hopefully. "Maybe they figure it ain't worth much. Well, let them think so! I know better!"

But even David did not know the real value of that farm! Even David did not know that, underground, where the old pioneer cabin had once stood, there lay buried a fortune in gold!

CHAPTER XII

THE SELLING

Mother Harper's wish came true at last, and the men returned from Nebraska, but with bad news. They were not interested in the farm. They did not want to buy it.

So the Harpers' dream of moving away faded completely.

Father Harper found work in a St. Louis brewery, which was the largest brewery in the whole country. But its great size did not help Father Harper at all, because his job was probably the smallest!

Then, at last, something quite unexpected happened. Just as Father Harper was starting to work one morning, the postman brought a letter to the door. It was a special

delivery letter and it came from Omaha, Nebraska.

"Well, I declare!   It's from Aunt Sophie!"
cried Father Harper, opening it quickly.

"What does it say?" asked the children, in
a chorus.   And Father Harper began to
read:

"DEAR BROTHER:
*You will be surprised to hear from me, but
that has nothing to do with what I am going
to say! I am going to offer you a handsome
fortune if that headstrong son of yours will
return to me! I was mortified when he ran
away from my home—the little alligator!—
and I am more than ever determined to bring
him up as a gentleman! As you well know,
a Harper never accepts defeat! So send the
little scamp back at once and I will send you
all the money you want.*

Your sister,
SOPHIE."

"All the money you want!" Why, mercy, thought Mother Harper, now they could do anything—could go anywhere! They could take Dot away from the smoky city, away from the coming winter's cold!

"This time," said Mother Harper, "David will have to go to Aunt Sophie's. There's not a mite of help for it!"

Father Harper did not answer. He was looking sadly out of the window at the big city. He was hearing it humming its busy tunes. And, all at once, he remembered an old courthouse, which stands in St. Louis.

Before the Civil War, slaves were sold at this courthouse and the stone auction block is still there.

Today, people do not sell other people. Yet, suddenly, it had occurred to Father Harper that this was exactly what they were planning to do! Planning to sell David to Aunt Sophie!

CHAPTER XIII

THE FAILURE

The weather turned cold and snow began to fall, so that soon the big, flat country was covered to its neck in its white winter overcoat.

But snow and sleet and ice could not stop the farmers. Cattle and hogs must be fed; work must go on, on the farm.

In great boots, David walked back and forth over the frozen ground. The sky was sad and gray most of the day and there were no bird songs.

It was good to come out of the cold, into Mrs. Thompson's warm kitchen each evening, to smell hot biscuits baking, and to stand by the stove, toasting numb fingers.

After supper, Farmer Thompson read his

Courtesy of Kansas City Southern Ry. Company

A TRAIN CARRYING FREIGHT FROM KANSAS CITY,
MISSOURI, TO THE GULF OF MEXICO

farm journals and the free papers sent out
by the university, while David toiled over
school lessons.   Every night he fell asleep
to the sound of coyotes howling as they
roamed the country in search of food.   He
fell asleep, too, with a promise in his strong,
young arms—a promise of work on his
father's farm next spring.

In the morning, the little white, country
schoolhouse, with its peaked roof, clanged a
bell.   David had to get up early in order to

complete his chores before the long walk to school.

He liked school well enough, but he preferred the lectures to which Farmer Thompson occasionally took him. These were by a county farm adviser, who gave his eager audience wonderful new ideas about the farm.

It was all right, thought David, to learn geography; to learn such things as that Topeka is the capital of Kansas and Little Rock, of Arkansas.

But to know how to cure cattle when they fell ill, or the right way to spray fruit trees —well, those were matters of much more importance to David!

He vowed that nobody should ever take him away from the country again. Whenever he recalled his visit to Aunt Sophie's he shuddered with horror.

He seldom heard from the family in St. Louis. Even Dot's letters were not so fre-

Courtesy The St. Louis Globe Democrat

THE OLD COURTHOUSE IN ST. LOUIS, MISSOURI—ON ITS STEPS SLAVES WERE SOLD AND IN ONE OF ITS ROOMS THE DRED SCOTT DECISION WAS WRITTEN.

quent any more. But one day, upon his return from school, he found one awaiting him.

Dot wrote nothing about the family's poverty, nor about her illness; nor did she mention Aunt Sophie's letter. For Mother and Father Harper had decided that they could not force David to go to Omaha; that they could not sell their son!

Dot did say, however, that Father Harper had lost his job in the brewery, and had gone traveling as a salesman. He had been away from his family all winter long.

He had crossed the State of Missouri, stopping in Jefferson City, with its handsome capitol building standing on a hill.

He had gone to Booneville, which is filled with memories of the famous pioneer, Daniel Boone, and where the first steamer up the Mississippi landed. Then on to St. Joseph, where a monument marks the starting point of the Pony Express.

He had visited Lincoln, capital of Nebraska, and Omaha, the largest city. He had crossed a bridge to Omaha's twin city, Council Bluffs, Iowa, which claims more railroad stations and grade crossings than any other in the world.

Finally, he had reached Sioux City, Iowa, in the center of a rich farming district, busy with her many industries.

And now Father Harper was on his way back to St. Louis. He was sitting in a railway train, looking out the window at the many welcome signs of approaching spring. He could hardly wait to see his family again.

At the door of his flat, he was met by his oldest son. The tall and lanky Bill wore one of his mother's aprons and held a long spoon in his hand.

The baby was crying in his high-chair. Ted and Tess were screaming and pulling each other's hair on the floor. The room was in a state of frightful disorder and smelled of burned food.

"Well, land sakes!" cried Father Harper. "What's the matter here? Where's your ma?"

Almost at once, Bill's expression told him that something terrible had happened. The boy licked his lips nervously and it was plain that he disliked breaking this unpleasant news to his father.

"Well, Pa—" he began, "you see, Dot's been feeling poorly of late, and today—"

Just then, Tess let out a hideous howl of rage, and Bill picked her up by the seat of her baggy, little bloomers. He set her down firmly in a chair. Then he did the same thing to Ted, plumping him on a couch across the room.

"You two leave be!" he scolded. "Can't you see I've got my hands full with the supper?"

"But Bill—" cried the distracted Father Harper. "Where's Dot? Where's your mother?"

Courtesy of Kansas City Southern Ry. Company

IN THE OZARKS NEAR NOEL, MISSOURI

"At the hospital," answered Bill. "The doctor came today and he took Dot away. Ma went along."

Father Harper waited only long enough to learn the name of the hospital. Then he rushed away, and soon he was standing with his wife by the bedside of their little girl.

They were listening to the doctor telling them that Dot must have long months in the sunshine and fresh air or she would never get well.

"She should go to the mountains," he finished. "Perhaps the Ozarks, for they are a natural health resort. The out-of-doors is the only thing that will save her life."

Dot, who lay in a sort of dream, heard this and murmured, "Oh, I do want to go to the Ozarks! I've read ever so much about them. They're filled with clear, cool streams, and trees and—and birds—"

"Hush, dear," whispered her Mother. "You'll be going there soon."

But Dot was feverish and she went on talking in her dream.

"I read," she continued, "that, in the Ozarks, they made a lake—the very biggest lake in all the world. I do want to see it; and the beautiful caves, too, like fairy palaces. They say there's a pool in one of them with fish that have no eyes—"

Her voice trailed off; she fell asleep at last, and Mother and Father Harper tiptoed out of the room.

That evening, they wrote two letters; one to Aunt Sophie in Omaha; the other to David, on the Thompson farm.

Aunt Sophie had won at last!

CHAPTER XIV

THE PLOWING

Just as soon as the frost was out of the ground, David began to plant a vegetable garden of his own on his father's farm.

He planned to open a roadside stand and to sell his fresh tomatoes, beans, lettuce and beets to passing motorists. With the money, he would buy seed and fertilizer. He would start to rebuild the old farm.

He had decided to plant his garden down by the cottonwood trees, in the very spot where his Grandfather's cabin had once stood. In the very spot where, underground, there still lay buried a fortune in gold.

Today, after school, he hurried through his chores and Mrs. Thompson, peeling po-

DAVID AT WORK

tatoes on the back step, watched him going down the road.

He was whistling as he drove the old horse hitched to an even older plow, which Farmer Thompson had loaned him. A happy youngster, thought Mrs. Thompson! And, all at once, she remembered the letter which had come from St. Louis that morning.

She stood up and called, "Davie! Oh, Davie, there's a letter here for you!" But David did not hear her. He continued on his way.

"Oh, well," thought Mrs. Thompson. "It can wait, I expect."

She glanced at the name on the back of the envelope. It was from his parents. Likely just news of the family and not very important.

Mrs. Thompson could hardly have guessed that this letter meant the end of poor David's happiness, his hopes and his plans! That it meant departure from the farm and a return to Aunt Sophie's, if he were to save his sister's life.

So she placed the letter on the kitchen table to await David's return at supper time.

The afternoon glowed warmly. The country sent out a blossom-perfumed breath, as

David's plow turned up thick rolls of earth.

A tiny breeze stirred in the cottonwood trees. David liked to remember that this was the very place where another David had started his farm so long ago.

All about, the land was opening fresh, green eyes and hope flowed through every part of it. It was recovering from its weather-beating and new homesteads were springing up everywhere.

David watched the sun sinking lower and he knew that it was time to stop work and go home. But he could not seem to tear himself away and kept repeating, "Just one more row—"

Then, suddenly, his plow struck something hard in the ground. He stopped the horse and climbed down from his high seat.

"Rock!" frowned the great-grandson of David Harper the First. "Pesky old rock!" And he kicked at the soil which covered that pioneer gold.

Courtesy of International Harvester Company

A MODERN DAIRY FARM

"There's no sense starting to dig out rock now," he thought. "Too late. The folks'll be waiting supper."

He pushed back his straw hat and wiped his hot forehead with a large bandanna handkerchief. He turned the horse's head.

"Git along, Jess," he said. "Tomorrow we'll come back and tussle with it."

But there would be no tomorrow on the

farm for David if he went back to Thompson's now. If he went back and found that letter from his family he would be on his way to Aunt Sophie's tomorrow!

Perhaps the old sun knew this and felt sorry for the earnest little farmer. At any rate, as David turned, the warm, kind sun shot a gleam upon the ground and it caught his eye. He pulled in the reins and stopped. He went back and—picked up a golden nugget!

Where had this come from? Nobody owned gold like this nowadays. Why, it looked—

An idea, almost too strange to believe, flashed across David's mind. He kicked once more at the earth. Rocks? Maybe not! Maybe it was—

He began to dig like a frantic dog after a bone.

Later on, the sun went sinking out of sight, with a proud smile on his face. He had watched David pull out the last of his grandfather's gold!

When David arrived at the Thompson farm, his employers were just finishing supper.

"You're late, Davie," said Farmer Thompson. But he said it with an understanding smile. "How's the plowin' getting on?"

Before David could answer, however, Mrs. Thompson handed him the letter which had arrived that morning from St. Louis.

"From your folks," she said. "Sure hope it's good news."

"Much obliged, ma'am," said David.

He took the letter and after he had finished it, he handed it back to Mrs. Thompson.

"Read it, please, ma'am," he said, and Mrs. Thompson did.

When she came to the end of the Harpers' sad story, her face was full of pity.

"Why, Davie!" she said. "This is dreadful!

And it means that you'll be leavin' us, too!"

"No, ma'am, it doesn't!" said David unexpectedly.

The Thompsons questioned him with their eyes. Would he refuse to go to the aid of his sick sister? It did not sound like David!

"I'm not goin' to leave these parts— ever," he went on. "Though I expect I'll be moving over next door soon's I get the new house built!"

Farmer Thompson looked at David as though he thought the boy had lost his senses.

"Moving next door?" he asked. "Building a house? What in thunderation are you talkin' about, Davie?"

"Well, you see, sir," said David calmly, "I'm going to put up a house on Pa's farm— a great big one. And a barn, and two silos, to store plenty of feed for all the stock I'm aimin' to keep."

Perhaps David had been sun-struck! But

Courtesy of University of Nebraska

UNIVERSITY OF NEBRASKA, AGRICULTURAL ENGINEERING
BUILDING

no, it was not yet hot enough for that. And, besides, Farmer Thompson knew that David was used to being out in all kinds of weather. What was the matter with him?

"We'll all be moving back to the farm again," he continued easily. "Only first, of course, Dot'll have to head for those mountains—What do you call 'em? The Ozarks. Yep, so she'll get good and strong before—"

"Land of mercy!" cried Mrs. Thompson. "What's ailin' him?"

David laughed and took her by the hand.

"Come along with me, ma'am," he said. "And you, too, sir. I want to show you both something."

He led the astonished Farmer Thompson and his wife out of the house.

But how much more astonished were these two good people when they saw what David had to show them out in the yard—when they saw David's precious gold!

A few days later Aunt Sophie tore open a letter, which she had just snatched from the hand of her frightened maid. She smiled in a satisfied way as she began to read it.

"Ah, now," she chuckled, "now we shall see when the little rattlesnake is coming back to me! It had better be soon. Let me see—ah, let me s—"

She stopped reading rather abruptly, and the satisfied smile turned into a frightful scowl.

"Why—why—what does this say?" she cried furiously. "What does this mean? He isn't coming? The little hop-toad isn't coming at all? And they are returning my money, because they don't need it since David found—"

But, at this point, Aunt Sophie could bear it no longer. Her face turned a bright purple, and she sat down so hard that she broke the chair and went sprawling on the floor in an undignified heap!

CHAPTER XV

THE HARVEST

Today, David Harper the Third is one of the most successful farmers in the Middle West. He is also one of the most modern. For, David went to one of the great agricultural colleges and learned all about modern farming.

He has put this knowledge to use, and now just look at the old farm! No one would ever know it!

There are acres and acres of wheat and corn fields, which stretch away like a feathery sea. Wild roses grow about a fence that circles a pretty, white farmhouse, and near by is an orchard bright with flaming fruit.

David is standing on the porch. He is

shading his eyes with his hand, because an automobile is driving up to the entrance and he is wondering who it can be.

Imagine David's astonishment when a mountain of flesh and rustling silk steps out of that automobile and he recognizes Aunt Sophie! She appears larger, noisier and crosser than ever!

She greets David with a snort. He takes her hand and leads her into the house.

Mother and Father Harper are a little bewildered by Aunt Sophie's visit. And so is David. But he laughs good-naturedly and asks:

"Why do you honor me with this visit, Aunt Sophie? I always thought you disliked small boys. You called them little rattlesnakes and complimentary things like that, I remember!"

Aunt Sophie glared. "You are not a small boy any longer!" she said. "You are a tall young man, and—" she hesitated. "And that is even worse!" she added tartly.

David threw back his head and laughed so loudly at this that pretty soon Aunt Sophie began to laugh with him.

"You were the spunkiest little kangaroo I ever met!" she wheezed, between chuckles. "And I did not dislike you at all! In fact, I missed you dreadfully when you left."

Then she told David and his parents the object of her visit. She had come to ask them for one of their children.

"I know you don't need the money now," she said. "But I—I'm very lonesome. Besides," she added most softly, for Aunt Sophie, "I promise to be kinder this time."

"But our children are grown up now," said Mother Harper, who was plump and rosy from a life of ease and comfort. "Bill runs a store in town and is doing very well. Ted and Tess are away at college and Dot's married to Farmer Thompson's boy. They live next door and—"

"What about the baby?" snapped Aunt Sophie impatiently. "He can't be grown up yet. Why, he must be about the same age as the little rattle—I mean, as David was when he came to live with me."

"I am! And I want to go to the city, too!" cried a voice, belonging to a sturdy boy with golden hair, who ran into the room. He went straight over to David.

"Please let me go to the city, Davie!" he plead. "I don't want to stay on the farm!"

David's face fell. "But I planned to send you to college, Buddy," he said. "Don't you want to learn all those wonderful new things they're teaching now, so you can help me on the farm some day?"

"Sure I do, Davie," answered the boy, and his deep blue eyes looked into his brother's muddy, tan ones. "But I think I can help you in the city as well. You see, I figure that if I go into business, I can sell the stuff you raise on your farm."

"So you shall! So you shall!" screamed Aunt Sophie, making everyone jump sky-high. "Why, you shall become manager of the Omaha Stockyards, and president of all the railroads, the King of the Aksarben, and—"

Then, suddenly, she stopped, and laughed. "But first," she said, "and best of all, you shall become my own boy!"

With that, a rather remarkable thing happened. Aunt Sophie drew Buddy toward her and kissed him. Yes, Aunt Sophie actually kissed a "little rattlesnake"!

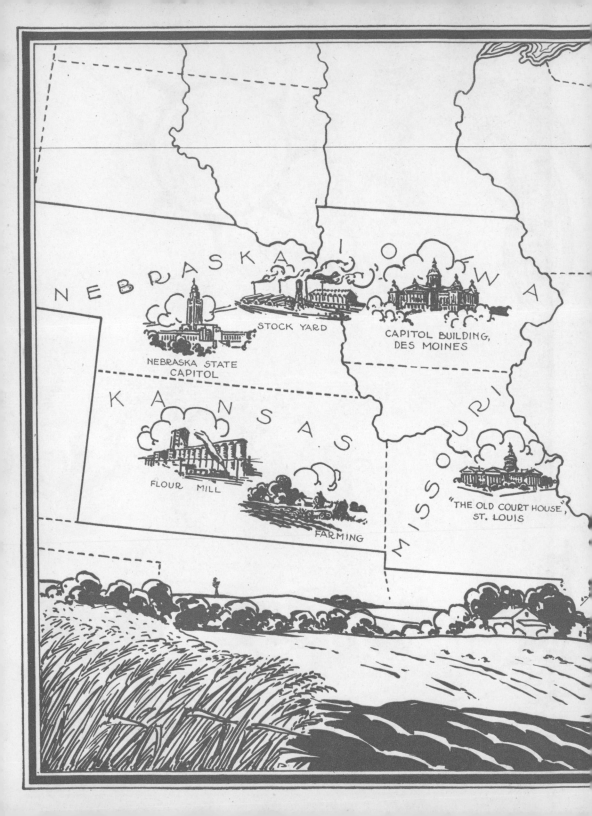

NEBRASKA

IOWA

KANSAS

MISSOURI

STOCK YARD

CAPITOL BUILDING,
DES MOINES

NEBRASKA STATE
CAPITOL

FLOUR MILL

FARMING

"THE OLD COURT HOUSE,"
ST. LOUIS